The Moonlight Smile that Stole my Heart

The Writer...his book...his love story

Kushal Singh

SAKA Productions Pvt Ltd

SAKA Productions

The characters and events portrayed in this book are fictitious. Any similarity to real persons, living or dead, is coincidental and not intended by the author.

ISBN-13: 9798410346122

Cover design by: Art Painter
Library of Congress Control Number: 2018675309
Printed in the United States of America

I love you and that's the beginning
and end of everything.
R SCOTT FITZGERALD

Contents

Introduction

A love story of a lonely writer takes the form of a bestseller novel. This is what best describes the book in one line. The love story of a young lonely writer Aditya and his love Ahana. Read to find out what happens when dreams of tomorrow force Ahana to leave her love of life behind. As the love story of Ahana and Aditya were progressing at its pace, time had its own plans. Ahana leaves for America to pursue her dancing career whereas, on the other hand, Aditya is back to where he started, his lonely life. Aditya's life takes a big turn as he goes on to become the most celebrated of the writers all over the globe when he decides to preserve his memories with Ahana in the form of a novel. Will the novel, "The Moonlight Smile that Stole my Heart" ever get to its complete end, or some stories are never meant to be completed. Will our Romeo writer Aditya ever again meet his Juliet Ahana? Read on to find out what destiny has for the love buds.

Chapter 1

The Beginning

My master is a 19-year-old boy who lives in the house as a tenant in a single room. He is very good at studies, a scholar, and an ambitious writer. But there is a fault too, he is a very shy person who can't make friends and that's the reason he has no friends in the new city even after spending two years here. Sorry, I forgot to tell you his name. His name is Aditya Sharma, a person who has always lived all alone, wakes up early completes his routine peacefully, and finally completes his ever so boring day.

One day when as usual I was marching with my master back to the room in his shirt's pocket, we saw a lot of cartons lying in the varanda but my master ignored it. As soon as he was about to open the room, a girl patted on his back and he suddenly got scared since he was in his sense of imagination and worries. He turned back and saw —a girl with brown hairs, a bright smile, and an admiring face that reflected a polite nature. The girl asked him for help in a polite manner. So, My master helped her in picking up the scattered things. After work, the girl thanked Aditya and offered him a handshake. With slight of nervousness, Aditya accepted the handshake. After a minute of introduction, I got to know that the girl's name was Ahana. This was when Aditya and Ahana met for the first time.

Chapter 2

The Current Scenario of Life

Ahana was another rentier in the house &; lived just 1 floor next to Aditya with her family which consisted of her mother father and a 10-year-old brother.

My master is a writer, writing novels is his passion. But unfortunately, he failed in getting them published, however, he was hopeful of them in the future. After 2-3 Novels, he started writing forcefully with no interest or feelings. His life is full of problems. The pressure of studies, financial problems, lack of friends or to be specific no friends, constantly losing interest in his writing, and most importantly that feeling of being alone. Aditya was a very shy boy who respected everyone, cared for everyone, and helped everyone. But he never shared anything with anyone, he was best in keeping his problems to himself.

Ahana was some way or the other similar to Aditya in nature but she knew how to make friends and so he had a lot of friends in her new college. She used to spend most of her time on the terrace studying, one of those habits which were similar to Aditya's.

Chapter 3

The Friend she needs

One day, when Aditya was studying at the terrace, suddenly Ahana came and asked Aditya if she could study there too. They both were studying in such a manner as if someone has banned speaking. But finally, the silence broke when Ahana started laughing in a low voice and Aditya looked at her. Ahana showed him a sentence that she misread and that's why it sounded funny. Now Aditya joined Ahana in laughing. Aditya was so shy that he didn't even laugh comfortably in front of her.

Now they started talking frequently in between, about everything around accept each other. Finally, Aditya saw the time and said Goodbye to Ahana and she also replied with a smile. The next morning, when Aditya went to the terrace to have a morning walk, he saw Ahana doing Yoga, and out of awkwardness, he was about to return from the stairs itself but suddenly Ahana spotted him and wished him Good morning. Aditya wished him good morning too and apologized for disturbing her. Ahana forced Aditya to sit beside her and join her in Yoga. Now you better know Aditya's nature, he was so nervous that it can't be expressed but he somehow gathered courage and joined her.

Things went like this many days, doing Yoga together, studying at the terrace, wishing each other, etc. A good foundation was already set for a good friendship.

One day Aditya saw Ahana sitting very sadly on the terrace thinking something. Aditya went close to her and asked if something has happened. But as expected she denied the fact that she is sad. That day Ahana wasn't speaking anything while studying and Aditya also wanted to give her some space. Now it was time for Aditya to go since it was already 10:15 p.m. He waited till now supposing that Ahana would tell him but it didn't happen. At last, Aditya said to her with calmness in his voice, “telling your problem or sharing your emotions won't lessen the burden on you but will lessen its effect”. He added, “any feeling, sad or happy, should be expressed to make space for new ones”. He smiled and turned to the stairs to go from there when suddenly Ahana stopped him and asked very confidently with a deep sense of expectations, "Can I always trust you to share all my feelings with, sad or happy, excited or nervous, any feeling, any thing?"

Aditya smiled and asked her patiently, "What do you think?" And she passed a satisfying smile that reflected her trust for him. Ahana looked towards the moon and the stars and held her head high for the moonlight to come and enlight her face, her smile glittering with the moonlight, did make a special space in Aditya's heart that day as he looked at her with an inner peace.

Chapter 4

From 'Aditya' to 'Adi'

One day when Aditya came back home, he heard some music being played on the speaker from Ahana's floor. When Aditya went upstairs, he saw a group of boys and girls. When he started climbing the stairs, he saw Ahana dancing with a boy, and then Aditya realized that some dance rehearsals were going on. Aditya came back to his room picking up his clothes from the terrace.

On the other hand, Ahana wasn't dancing comfortably and that's why her friends were pushing her to dance well and bring some chemistry to the act. Finally, Ahana stopped the rehearsal for a short break. She asked everyone to have a 10-minute break and then they would get back to practice.

When Ahana looked at the time, she knew that Aditya must be back home, so she went to his room to freshen up her mood with a short chit chat. This was the first time Ahana was going to Aditya's room. Ahana knocked softly ensuring he isn't asleep. Aditya opened the door and was a bit nervous since his room wasn't arranged properly. Noticing that Ahana is sweating, he brought her a glass of water. She thanked him and asked him about his day. Aditya replied politely, "like every other day". He asked Ahana how were her rehearsals going ? She told him disappointingly that she isn't comfortable performing since they are all very dangerous stunt steps that have to be performed with the support of your partner and she don't know why isn't she able to trust her partner even though he is a good friend of her. Aditya told her that he never performed anywhere on any occasion but can understand trust is must in these kinds of risky steps. A single doubt can cause a severe injury. Aditya saw Ahana smiling towards him, he asked, "What happened?" Ahana remarked, "Just do me one favor, please come with me. I believe I would be able to perform better with you." He asked that why is it so, but Ahana didn't move a inch from her request and kept on pleading him. Finally, after a lot of no and please, Aditya agreed nervously.

Ahana went to her group and convinced them for performing with a new partner. Unwillingly the group agreed and the boy with whom she was dancing got annoyed.

When everyone saw Aditya, the first question everyone had in their mind was how will he perform such a bold act? Because one could easily tell how shy and introvert Aditya was. When the act started, the first try failed because Ahana was still scared. Now

Aditya looked into her eyes and asked her to just assume that it is only he and her who are present in the hall, to forget about every other thing. Ahana nodded her head and smiled. This time when they started no one would have ever expected that they would complete the act so smoothly and that too with such elegance. This time Ahana completed all her risky steps with confidence. Everyone started hooting.

After the performance, Aditya was moving back to his room when Ahana stopped him on the stairs and thanked him for helping her out with the dance. Aditya congratulated her and wished her luck for the act. Ahana stopped him again and asked him politely, "If you don't mind, can I call you Adi? Aditya seems a bit formal and I don’t think we need to be formal with each other" At first, Aditya hesitated but then replied with a smile, "Of course, you can".

Chapter-5

The Bigger Problem

One day when Aditya came back home and went to the terrace to take his clothes, there he saw Ahana sleeping on the chair with her eyes red and wet. Aditya someway or the other assumed that Ahana was crying as it looked like.

He shook her slightly and called her name. Finally, she was awake. Aditya asked her if she was crying but as expected she denied and wrapped the topic by asking, "So, how was your day?"

After fifteen minutes, when Aditya started moving back to his room, Ahana waved him a bye and he did the same but somewhere he knew that she was crying and was determined to know the reason.

The same night when Aditya was cooking his meal, he heard some patting of steps from the stairs. Out of curiosity, he went to the terrace, and now here comes the reason for his curiosity. When he first entered the terrace, he didn't see anyone. But while returning he heard some crying and he stopped. Now he realized that Ahana hid behind the door. Aditya quickly turned the door and found her crying with her hands on her mouth trying to lower the voice of her crying. He asked her why is she crying in a tense way. She didn't reply but hugged him tightly and continued crying.

First of all, Aditya didn't do anything and let her cry for some time. After some time he was able to calm her down and then he asked for the reason politely. And this time before she could make any excuses, he asked her to answer truthfully in a serious way. After some deep breaths, she started telling Aditya the whole scenario and after listening to the whole scenario Aditya was more shocked than sad. So let me tell you what the whole situation was. Ahana's parents died in a car accident so she didn't live with her parents but with her uncle and aunt. Today after an argument with them, they left the home as already they found her a financial burden on themselves. They abused her parents and that is why she was crying. She confirmed that they would not return. When Aditya questioned her that how can they leave their own house, she answered that they definitely can because it was not their own house. They too lived on rent as you and collected the rent from you to give it to the main owner of the house.

It took some time for Aditya to settle himself from the whole scenario and then he wiped Ahana's tears. He remarked, "It is now time for you to stay strong Ahana because your parents are watching all this and they would never want their daughter to be weak. It doesn't matter if they abused your parents because I can guarantee that your parents must have been just like you, kind and humble. So what the world says should not matter to you. Your personal opinion matters the most, if you think your parents were a blessing to you then they surely were and are even now. Life is not as easy as it looks. We are the warriors of our own lives and we'll have to win this battle and fight till the very end. So keep yourself strong my girl and forget everything that has happened earlier because now a bunch of problems is waiting for us so look forward to it." He asked her to take a rest since they have a lot of problems to deal with.

The word, “my girl”, seemed to do something special to Ahana.

She stopped Adi and asked, "How well do you know the solution to every problem that I have?" He replied, "Just a mere coincidence"

He sent Ahana back to her room and ordered strictly to sleep and not to wake up till the morning. Ahana smiled and followed her orders obediently.

Chapter 6

The test of survival

Ahana and Aditya are standing on the balcony. Both of them are just trying to figure out what should they do now. Adi asked Ahana if she knew the house owner's address. She disappointingly denied. He asked her to search for the tenant agreement in the house. Both of them started searching for it and finally, after two hours of hard toil, they found the owner's name, phone and most importantly the address. They took a sigh of relief but Ahana questioned Aditya about how will they give the rent. He asked her not to panic and let's meet the owner first.

They went to the landlord's house which was not very far. On reaching there, they found that the landlady was an old religious Christian lady which was reflected from her house.

Read the following conversation between the landlady and them.....

Aditya: Hello mam. If I am not wrong, you are Miss Rosy Robert?

Miss Rosy: Yes my child but how can I help you?

Ahana: Actually we live in that house which you gave on rent to Mr. Satendra Sharma, my uncle. And there is a problem.

Miss Rosy: Every problem has a solution my dear children, but first come in and let's have a cup of coffee.

(Ahana and Aditya looked at each other nervously)

Aditya: Sure mam.

(In the guest room)

Miss Rosy: Tell me, dear, what's the problem?

Ahana: Come on Adi, go ahead.

Aditya: Miss Rosy, the problem is that Mr. Satendra has left the house without informing you. And I and Ahana are currently living there.

Miss Rosy: Just a second young boy. How can they leave their daughter?

Ahana: Oh no ma'am they are not my parents.

Miss Rosy: Oh! I am sorry sweetheart.

Aditya: So we were thinking if you could give us some more time to pay you the rent.

Miss Rosy: That's completely fine dear. But how will you be able to pay the rent? Do you have any work?

Ahana: No mam, but we'll look for something.

Miss Rosy: (after thinking something deeply) I do have a solution dear. My husband and I run a small cafe. But these days my husband is not well. So you can take the charge of the cafe and keep all the earnings of your hard work. We will just come there for breakfast and if you wish you can donate a part of your earnings to our NGO. We run that cafe for our enjoyment so there will be no share from your profit, what you earn will be yours and then you can pay the rent. Will it be fine?

Ahana and Aditya: (together) That's awesome mam.

Aditya: I just don't know how to thank you. But still thank you very much, mam, seriously from the bottom of my heart.

Ahana: I just can't believe that there are still selfless people like you in this cruel world. Honestly, thank you, mam.

Miss Rosy: Don't say that my children, you both are like my son and daughter. By the way, you both look very good together.

(Ahana and Aditya look down and smile a bit)

Aditya: So should we leave? We have a lot of work to be done before going to the cafe.

Miss Rosy: Sure dear. Was lovely to meet you both.

Ahana: Same here ma'am.

Now both Ahana and Aditya are at home and they seem to be tired as well. Now it was time for dinner and both of them were in their respective rooms, sleeping soundly. Ahana woke up out of hunger and started calling Aditya. She called aloud his name.

Ahana: (calling aloud) Adi! where are you?

Aditya: Coming.

(He goes to her floor)

Aditya: What happened?

Ahana: I am hungry very much.

Aditya: So what should we eat?

Ahana: I don't have anything to eat.

Aditya: A food has to be prepared and then eaten but the question is what should we make?

Ahana: Anything.

Aditya: Let me check the market and then I shall suggest.

Ahana: Shall I accompany you?

Aditya: Up to you.

Ahana: Sure, let's go.

They both return from the market with some

vegetables and kitchen essentials. They have started preparing for the dinner. Ahana brings the speaker to the hall and plays some songs. Ahana loves dancing and so she is enjoying herself in the kitchen however it is too hot there. She makes Adi dance with her as well.

Chapter -7

Daily Life & The Twist

It's early morning and my Master, as well as Ahana, are in their respective schools.

Friend – So, what's the plan for Rohan's birthday party tonight?

Ahana – Sorry guys. I am not coming to the party tonight. I really can't. I have some important work to be done tonight at home.

Friend – Are you sure, you are not coming?

Ahana – Yeah, really some important work at home, and please apologize to Rohan on behalf of me.

Friend – Fine!!

Ahana's school is over and she is on her way to the cafe from home. On reaching the cafe, she sees Aditiya and a girl talking happily outside the cafe.

Ahana – (calling aloud) Adi!!

Aditya – I think I should leave, bye. Coming Ahana!

Ahana – (angrily) Don't we have work inside?

Aditya – Of course, we do have.

(Ahana gives a straight look to the girl there)

(In The Cafe)

Aditya – I have got some essential things but I don't think we need them right now.

Ahana – I have too got something for you and me.

Aditya – What ?

Ahana – Aprons!!

Aditya – That looks really professional.

Suddenly someone enters the cafe and asks for a cold coffee. Aditya prepares the coffee and Ahana takes it to the man.

Ahana – Your coffee sir.

Man – You both look very young. Part time work here?

Ahana – (smiling) Kind of.

Man – I am a regular customer here. My name is Dhruv Biswa. Your good name?

Ahana – Myself Ahana. A pleasure to meet you, sir.

Dhruv – Me too.

(Ahana goes back to the counter)

Ahana – I think I should look for the juicer inside.

Aditya – Sure.

(It is a dark room connected to the kitchen and Ahana picks up a stool and stands looking for the juicer on the top shelf. Suddenly the stool starts to tumble and Ahana is about to fall behind but, coincidently Aditya reaches there and saves Ahana by holding her back.)

Aditya – What are you doing?

Ahana – I didn't know that the stool tumbles.

Aditya – You go now, I'll find the juicer.

(Finally, the day is about to end and the cafe is about to get closed, not very many customers today but still satisfying for the first day. A small kid enters the cafe and calls Aditya secretly)

Kid – I want to have a sandwich but I only have 10 Rs and my mum has given me this 10 Rs for buying a pencil.

Aditya – (Smiles) Wait for 10 minutes and I shall have a solution for you.

Kid – Can I sit here?

Aditya – Of course, Dear.

(Aditya goes to the kitchen and takes out the bread to make a sandwich.)

Ahana – Are you hungry?

Aditya- Yes, but this is not for me, it's for the kid sitting over there.

Ahana – Ohh.

(The sandwich is ready and Ahana takes it to the kid.)

Kid – It's yum, so cheesy. Thank you very much for this.

(After eating, the kid calls Aditya and gives him 10 Rs.)

Aditya – Do you have siblings?

Kid – Yes, a small sister.

Aditya – (smiles and takes out 20 Rs from his pocket and handovers it to the kid)

Aditya – Buy yourself a pencil and chocolate for your sister. Understood?

Kid – (shakes his head joyfully and runs away) Bye-Bye!!

Aditya – (loudly) Carefully!!

(Ahana watches all this from the counter and smiles.)

(They have closed the cafe and are now moving back home.)

Ahana – The weather is nice and windy. Shouldn't we walk back home?

Aditya – Yup. Why not?

Ahana – (while walking) I was wondering that we were fortunate today since we only had customers for coffee, tea, sandwiches and toast only. But what about the pizzas and burgers; we don't know how to make them.

Aditya – YouTube; the teacher in every problem.

Ahana – (laughs) Sure, just like you.

Days pass and Ahana and Aditya's life is going smoothly. School in the morning and café in the afternoon. Ahana has to go to her dance class so she leaves the café at 5 pm and returns back at 7:30 pm. She never wanted Aditya to toil alone but Aditya doesn't want her to leave her dance classes; giving her the satisfaction that he doesn't have any problem in handling the cafe alone, he sends her to the dance classes. The cafe is running well. They have reduced the cost of food items they have recently learned to make like pizzas and burgers. Mrs. Rosy and her husband gives a visit to the café every Sunday to see how things are working out.

But one Monday evening, it was 8:15 and Ahana didn’t return from her dance classes yet. It has also started raining for a while. Aditya is tense about this. He calls Ahana but she isn't picking up the call. Now he is worrying more than before. He can't go to her dance academy as there are still few customers in the cafe, he continues with his work giving himself a positive opinion on the situation.

Now, after 30 minutes, when all the customers are gone and still there is no answer to the calls, Aditya is getting more worried. He can't take all this and decides to go and check. It's still raining outside. There is no public transport available at the time, so Aditya borrows a bike from his neighborhood general store. The man being generous gives him the keys.

On reaching the academy, the receptionist tells him to visit the room inside. Entering the room, he found 2-3 girls standing in a hurdle, he asks them about Ahana and suddenly he hears the voice ,"Adi". This gives him a sigh of relief. He turned back and found Ahana crying. He rushes towards the chair where she is sitting and as soon as he reaches, Ahana hugs him tightly while crying. Making Ahana sit properly, he asked her what had happened to her. Ahana's friends tell him that her ankle was twisted badly during the rehearsals due to which she is in a lot of pain. Aditiya calms her down first and then explains to Ahana that if she wants to dance again she would have to see a doctor immediately. Ahana agrees and tries to walk on one leg supporting herself by Aditya's hand and shoulder. Her friends appreciated Aditya since they were trying to explain the same thing but were rather unsuccessful. At last, somehow Ahana manages to reach the bike. Then Aditya takes her to the doctor after which she got proper treatment and was a bit relieved from pain.

(while riding back home)

Ahana – You were worried?

Aditya – Definitely.

Ahana – I am sorry.

Aditya – It's ok. But you should have called me at least.

Ahana – Yaa! I know, but I was not in my state of mind.

Aditya – I know. Now from today itself no café, no dance academy for 10-15 days. Mark my words.

Ahana – I can't leave the café on you alone.

Aditya – You don't trust me?

Ahana – Of course, I do. But I will come with you to the café and no more debate on this topic.

Aditiya – Fine, but you won't do anything there and there's no debate on that. That's it.

Ahana – (sadly) Okk!!

(Aditya and Ahana are back home. Aditya is icing Ahana's ankle and she has a bit of pain.)

Aditya – Fortunate you are, that it's not a fracture, just a swelling.

Ahana- Hmm. How was the day at the cafe?

Aditya - Good. Plenty of customers to handle.

Ahana – That's great.

Aditya is walking back to his room, suddenly Ahana calls him

Ahana – (calling aloud) Adi!!!

Aditya – What happened?

Ahana – I was wondering if you could stay here only. I mean it's still raining and your room's roof must be leaking. Plus I might need help anytime.

Aditya – Oh, no-no you don't worry I am completely fine there. I will manage. And you can call me whenever you need anything.

Ahana – I am not asking you, I am telling you. You will stay here and that's final. No more arguments.

Aditiya – Ok- ok fine, now don't get angry. Obeying your orders mam. Happy?

Ahana- (smiling) Very happy.

Like always, days passed and everything went smoothly. Ahana is better but still hasn't recovered completely. Aditya stays with her on the same floor in the room next to hers. The good thing is that Aditya has started writing again. Today there will be a surprise for Ahana. Let's see what it is.

(In The Cafe)

Ahana's mobile rings but Ahana is not there, she

is in the kitchen. Aditya doesn't want to pick up her phone but it looks important since it is ringing again so he answers the call.

Aditya – (on phone) Yes!

Girl – Ahana?

Aditya – Oh no, this is Aditya speaking. Ahana is currently not here. I'll tell her about the call as soon as she comes. If there is anything urgent, then you can tell me, I'll pass the message?

Girl – Aditya, this is Priya, Ahana's friend. I wanted to ask her if we could visit your cafe and taste your burgers and coffee. If you don't mind.

Aditya – Oh, why not. We'll be glad to serve you.

Priya – That's great. Don't tell Ahana and let it be a surprise for her.

Aditya – (chuckles) Sure.

(35 minutes later)

Ahana and Aditya are standing at the counter having a chat. Suddenly Ahana's friends arrive there. She gets surprised seeing them. Aditya smiles in reply to Priya's thumbs up.

Ahana – You knew it?

Aditya – I think yes.

Ahana – Then why didn't you tell me?

Aditya – Surprise. Go, join them. Leave up the orders

on me. Don't worry.

Ahana – But...

Aditya – Just go.

Ahana and her friends are talking and laughing. Suddenly Aditya comes with the menu card.

Aditya – Here are the menu card ladies. Call me when you decide on your order and don't worry about any cost issues. Take it as a treat from Ahana.

Priya – That's really sweet of you Aditya. Thank you.

Aditya – Your welcome, I should leave.

(A few minutes later Ahana comes back to the counter after receiving orders from her friends. Read the conservation between her friends when she is absent.)

Shreya – Do you know Abhishek, that handsome boy in college has some serious feelings for Ahana?

Priya – Yeah. I heard of this.

Kirti – Why your reaction is so dull?

Priya – I don't know but I think Ahana likes Aditya.

Kirti – Maybe. And they look good together too. Cute perfect couples.

Shreya – That's true.

(Suddenly Ahana comes to the table with the food.)

Ahana – What happened guys? Talking very low?

Priya – Nothing. Just like that.

Aditya is busy with some work and Ahana is talking to her friends when two boys enter the cafe and ask for the menu.

Aditya – Coming sir, just a minute.

Ahana – (shouts from her table) Leave it, Adi.

(Ahana goes to the counter and then handovers the menu. One of the boys touches Ahana intentionally. But she ignores them, thinking it was a mistake. Adi is also observing all this. Ahana returns back to the counter.)

Aditya – Any problem?

Ahana – (hesitatingly) No. Not really.

Aditya is observing that the boys are continuously staring at Ahana and her friends. They call Ahana again for giving the order. Ahana goes there and one of the boys touches her again, but Ahana is still not reacting, just ignoring. But Aditya has spotted it again and he looks really serious. Aditya leaves the counter and goes to them.

Aditya – Either you two leave the café or I'll have to take action.

Boy – What are you talking about man?

Ahana – (seeing Aditya in anger) Leave it, Adi.

Aditya – I said get out or I will have to take some

action.

(Everyone in the café is looking towards them since Aditya has raised his voice.)

Boy – Oh now I got it, so you are having a problem while we are touching the girl.

(Aditya loses his patience, he punches the boy hard and the boy falls to the ground. Now the argument has turned into a physical fight between Aditya and the two boys. There's not much people in the cafe. Ahana is really scared. She runs and calls some help from outside. Although, they were two and Aditya was alone. He has got them down on the floor and it looks like they are not going to stand up again. A police constable comes with Ahana but till then the fight was over and Aditya has had a bit of injury on his face and shoulders. The police constable takes both the boys out and appreciates Aditya for giving them the right result. Ahana looks at Aditya's condition and starts crying. Aditya goes inside in order to relax alone. Ahana's friends are also gone. Ahana rushes inside to see Aditya. He is holding his right shoulder and trying to take a deep breath. Suddenly Ahana enters in a hurry and hugs Aditya while crying. He is confused about what to do but Ahana is still crying)

Aditya – Ahana, are you fine?

Ahana – Shut up, don't speak anything!!

Aditya – But what happened?

Aditya holds Ahana's shoulders and calms her patiently. Wipes the tears in her eyes.

Ahana – What was the need of becoming a hero there?

Aditya – Yeah. I should have called a director and an actress too.

Ahana – (chuckles) Stupid! Wait here until I bring the first aid.

Ahana brings the first aid, smoothly applies the ointment over his injury, and covers his head with the bandage.

After a few days, everything is normal like always, Ahana has recovered but still hasn't started dancing. It's midnight and Aditya is studying in his room. Suddenly Ahana knocks on the door. He opens the door and finds her standing with a cake brightened up with candles.

Ahana – (smiling) Happy Birthday Adi!!!

Aditya – Thank you very much, but what's the date today?

Ahana – It's 29th August, your birthday. How can you forget that?

Aditya – Now I remember but how did you find that?

Ahana – Doesn't matter.

Aditya – Ok.

Ahana – Let's cut the cake.

Aditya – Sure.

(Aditya cuts the cake and feeds Ahana with his hands. She clicks some pictures and starts dirtying Aditya's face with the cake. He tries to escape but there is no running from her. Ahana posts the pictures on social media.)

(Next Morning)

Aditya – Let's go.

Ahana – But where are we going?

Aditya – Cafe, of course.

Ahana – Not at all. I am not coming to the cafe on your birthday and nor you are going.

Aditya – But why?

Ahana – What why? We'll celebrate your birthday. Let's plan something.

Ahana and Aditya are sitting idle in the living room. Ahana is thinking of what to do for Aditya's birthday while he is busy reading a novel.

Ahana – Get ready!!

Aditya – Where?

Ahana – Shopping.

Aditya - No Ahana. Not Shopping. I find it money waste.

Ahana – Then waste some money on your birthday. No more arguments.

Aditya – Fine.

Ahana – And wear your black cheque shirt.

Aditya – Why so?

Ahaan – Because I like it. You look good in it.

Aditya – Ok. Any other order mam?

Ahana – (chuckles) No.

Ahana and Aditya go to the city mall for shopping. He is standing idle while she is looking for shirts and T-shirts for him.

Ahana – (showing a shirt) How's it?

Aditya – Nice.

Ahana – Then go and try it.

Aditya comes out of the trial room wearing the shirt. Ahana gets surprised after seeing Aditya.

Aditya – Ahana? How do I look?

Ahana – Wait one photo is a must here. Come on smile Adi, you are looking damn hot.

Aditya – Really?

Ahana – I'm serious.

Ahana and Aditya go to the counter to purchases the shirt.

Ahana – I was wondering if you like movies or not?

Aditya – Not really. But can surely watch if it is good.

Ahana – What about a suspense thriller?

Aditya – Sure, I love suspense thrillers.

(3 hours later)

Ahana and Aditya come out of the auditorium after the movie.

Ahana – Adi I am hungry.

Aditya – So let's have something.

Aditya and Ahana had dinner in a restaurant and are now in a cab on their way back home.

Ahana – Adi, don't you expect any gift from me?

Aditya – You made my birthday special and fun. That's more than a gift for me. Nothing else required.

Ahana – (giving him the gift) But I have still got something for you.

Aditya – What it is?

Ahana – Open it.

Aditya unwraps the gift and finds a pen and a photo frame inside, there is a card too. The photo frame inside has a photo of Aditya and Ahana wearing aprons in the café and smiling with a coffee.

Aditya – It's so beautiful! I loved it.

Ahana – Remember this photo? We clicked when we entered the café for the first time. The pen is not for usual purpose. Use it on special occasions. I have sought luck and blessing from God for you in it and read the card before you go to sleep.

Aditya – Thank you very much. You know I never thought that I could be this much happy on my birthday.

Ahana – I'm glad that I was successful in making your day.

Aditya- You surely were.

Ahana and Aditya reaches home. They both head straight towards their rooms after wishing each other good night.

Aditya gets back to its room and keeps the card gifted by Ahana on the table. He places the frame smoothly on the lamp table near his bed after which he goes to the washroom and when he comes back he realizes that he had left the window open and it's quite airy outside. He searches for the letter but couldn't find it. The search has now been over an hour, throwing things here and there but he couldn't find it. Ahana knocks on the door and Aditya opens it.

Ahana - Why aren't you sleeping?

Aditya – I can't find my card.

Ahana – (hesitatingly) You read it?

Aditya – No, not yet.

Ahana – (hesitating) Aa... leave it, Adi, it was just a birthday card written happy birthday and a thought. Nothing important. You go and sleep.

Aditya – Are you sure?

Ahana – Trust me.

Aditya – (sadly) Fine.

Ahana – Good night.

Aditya – Good night.

Ahana comes out of the room, supports herself on the wall, and takes a big sigh of relief as if something horrible was going to happen.

Ahana- (to herself) Thank God, that Adi didn't read the letter.

Chapter - 8

Is It The End?

It's a very important day for Ahana as she has her national finals of the 'Dream Dance Championship'. Ahana and Aditya have reached the town hall for the finals on their newly bought scooty.

Aditya goes to the green room just before Ahana's performance to encourage her and as expected, Ahana was worried as well as nervous.

Ahana – No Adi No!! I can't perform.

Aditya – Relax... Relax. Sit here.

Ahana – But Adi.

Aditya – Sit.

Aditya – (tying her shoe lays) You are not here by luck or virtue, you are here because you have worked hard for this. If you don't win today, you'll forget it after a few days but if you don't give your 100%, then you'll regret your whole life. So don't dance to win, dance to express yourself, dance because you are a born dancer. So go and do what you know the best. I should leave or will miss the performance. All the best!!

(Aditya is going from the room, suddenly Ahana stops him.)

Ahana – Adi!

Aditya – What happened?

Ahana – Thank you!

Aditya – (smiles and wishes her the best of luck.)

After the performances, it was now time for the results. Ahana is standing on the stage with four more contestants.

Anker – So after 6 days of energetic and brilliant performances, the time has come for which these 5 contestants have been waiting for. A real tough choice for our judges but with the help of your votes they have reached the final decision.

And the winner of 'DDC' is.......... Ahana!!!

After listening to her name, Ahana opens her eyes and is in shock. She can't believe that she has won.

After the awarding ceremony, Ahana comes out with the trophy and hugs Aditya happily.

They both go for having ice cream to celebrate the win.

(2 days later)

Ahana and Aditya are in the cafe. Aditya is doing some calculations while Ahana is using her mobile. Suddenly Ahana receives a mail after which she shouts loudly "Adi!!".

Aditya – (in a scared voice) What happened, why are you shouting?

Ahana – (showing the email) Read this, "Congratulation Miss Ahana Srivastava you have been chosen by our team for a 3-year dance training under world-class dance experts of American Royal Dance Institute in New York.

Your tickets will reach you in 2 days. Keep your bags packed, in case you don't want to act on the opportunity, just call on this number 055-666-722.

Thank you!!

Aditya – This is sensational! I just can't believe this. Congrats Ahana, your dream has come true.

Ahana – Yes-Yes. I can't believe this Adi, is it really true? I hope my eyes have not been mistaken.

Aditya – It is very true, Ahana.

Chapter - 9

!!Dreams of Tomorrow....Sacrifice of Today!!

Only two days are left, and the tickets will be in Ahana's hand which is nothing less than a dream for her. But Ahana is sitting sadly at the cafe counter. Aditya comes close to her and asks the reason. She says that she doesn't know the reason. Aditya asks her if she wants to go out and have fun but she denies it as she isn't really in mood.

To lighten up her mood, Aditya plays her favorite song on the speaker and asks her for a dance, firstly she denies but after some time she finally joins him to dance on her favorite romantic song. Finally, Ahana is smiling.

Ahana – Adi?

Aditya – Yes.

Ahana – Won't you miss me?

Aditya – What do you think?

Ahana – This is cheating, whenever I put up a difficult question, you return it to me. That's not fair. Now answer me sincerely.

Aditya – Yes, I will.

Ahana – Ok. Won't you ask me the same question?

Aditya – I already know the answer.

Ahana – (smiling) And what is it?

Aditya – You know it too.

Ahana – I must say, you are a real trickster.

Aditya – (laughs) Thank you.

Finally, the day came, when Ahana will be leaving for New York. Ahana and Aditya are at the airport. Aditya has come to see her off. Ahana is waiting for her friend who is also going to New York. After few minutes, her friend arrives and now she has to say goodbye to Aditya. She wanted to hug him but don't know what resisted her. Just shook her hands for the goodbye and Aditya replied to her with a fake smile. The flight takes off and so does Ahana's dream but what is left here is her incomplete story.

Chapter - 10

Glory & Fame Awaits Aditya

It has been 2 months and Aditya and Ahana haven't talked, due to an accident Aditya lost his phone and Ahana's number. All doors for them to stay in touch are closed now.

Aditya's routine is simple and that is from home to cafe and cafe to home. He stays in the cafe late night till 11.30 or more. It's not that he isn't normal. He has accepted the fact very well that he is all alone again. He writes something daily in his diary after the cafe or when the cafe is empty. One day in the evening when Aditya was in the cafe, a group of 7-8 boys and girls came from the nearby coaching center who visited the cafe daily during the lunch break. They went to Aditya straight away.

Aditya – What happened to you all? Ten minutes here before lunchtime. Bunking the class?

Karthik – Yup, but for a reason.

Smita – We want an answer from you.

Aman – Do you believe in love?

Aditya – Aa...... (hesitating) Yes, but why do you ask.

Suman – So, what do you think, does every love story reaches its perfect end or there are some that remain incomplete forever?

Akash – What is more important love or courier?

Aditya – See, first thing, every story has got an end but it is totally up to us about what we think about the end, what is our definition of perfection. And courier is very important.

Suman – Ok. But you didn't answer, which is more important love or courier.

Aditya – Am I a love guru? Don't ask me such questions. Take your seats till then I prepare your lunch. Come on move fast and don't mess up the chairs.

Everyone – (disappointingly) Fine.

I forgot to tell you about one very important thing. Six days after Ahana's departure, Aditya was setting things in his room when he found a card behind the cupboard and if you are predicting what I want to tell then you are right. It was Aditya's birthday card which he lost that day without reading and Ahana said that it was just a wish card. Let's read and see how much truth existed in Ahana's words that day.

From Ahana

To Someone Special

First of all a very happy birthday Adi. May you live to double that of me and achieve everything you deserve. On this special occasion of your birthday, I want to confess something and for this I have gathered a lot of courage. From the first day, when you came into my life, you have always been a really special friend. With whom I cried, with whom I laughed. Saw all the ups and downs of life with you. You always stood behind me in every situation. Now when I see you happy and smiling, I start smiling automatically. From the first day, I have always loved spending time with you in every situation of life. But in recent times, what I have discovered can affect our friendship but you have the right to know. I think I really love you, Adi. Your feelings might not be the same as mine but I have always prayed to god and will continue to pray for you, for your success, for your life. Whoever may be that lucky girl, whom you will choose, but you deserve the best in the world.

- With love from Ahana

(Back to present story)

The next day when Aditya was in the cafe, late at night, a man came in, looking nearly 29-30 years of age. Aditya is shocked to see him as he enters the cafe. The cafe was empty and the man came in.

Aditya – (in shock) “The” great Pratyush Ahuja.

Pratyush – What happened, brother.

Aditya – Sir, I am not wrong, you are the C.E.O of P.R.K Publishers, India's and Asia's biggest publishing house and you wrote the book , "Seven Wonders Of Heaven".

Pratyush - Well, looks like you know me very well.

Aditya - Whole India knows you, sir. Oh, I am really sorry that I didn't ask you to sit till now. Please, sir, have a seat.

Pratyush – Thank you, we'll talk, you don't worry, but the reason I am here is that I am hungry.

Aditya – Sorry sir. You just relax, till then I will prepare something for you.

Pratyush – Sure, do you have something to read.

Aditya – (after thinking for a minute) Well, I am a writer too, to be specific, an aspiring writer.

Pratyush – Which type of book are you writing?

Aditya – A love story, I can't specify its type.

Pratyush – Well, I don't really read love stories. But you give me the copy; I'll have a go through.

Aditya – (on seeing a famous novel on the counter) Well, leave it, you can read that novel. Because you don't like love stories, you'll not like it, it's non fictional, so it doesn't have much spice.

Pratyush – You give me the novel as well as your book. I'll manage.

Aditya – Fine.

(25 minutes later)

Aditya is plating the dish when he sees that Pratyush was reading his book very attentively and not the novel.

Aditya – Sir, the dinner is ready.

Pratyush – (no response)

Aditya – Sir!

Pratyush – (asking to wait) Give me 5 minutes.

Aditya – Sir, it will get cold and dry.

Pratyush – Let it be.

(Pratyush is still reading the book.)

(Finally, Aditya brings the food to the table and Pratyush starts his meal.)

Pratyush – (while eating) where is she?

Aditya – Who?

Pratyush – Your story's female lead.

Aditya – Maybe somewhere in New York or I don't know exactly.

Pratyush – What's the time, till the cafe will be open tomorrow?

Aditya – 11:00 - 11:30 pm

Pratyush – Ok. Thank you for the dinner.

Aditya – How much did you complete the book.

Pratyush – Thirteen, fourteen pages. Ok, bye. See you soon, good night.

Aditya - Good night sir.

Aditya says goodbye to him. He was happy that he met a star-like Pratyush Ahuja but was also certain that he might not have liked his book. He picked the copy and closed the cafe.

The next day it was 11:15 pm at night and it was raining heavily. Aditya was washing utensils in the cafe and the cafe was empty. Suddenly, he hears someone calling him. He comes out from the kitchen to the counter and sees Pratyush all wet.

Aditya – Sir! What are you doing here?

Pratyush – Give me a towel first.

Aditya – Ohh, yes, of course.

(Pratyush dries himself with the towel. Aditya is preparing coffee for Pratyush and himself when he sees Pratyush searching for something on and near the counter)

Pratyush – Where it is?

Aditya – What?

Pratyush – Your copy in which you wrote the story.

Aditya – (while offering the coffee) Leave that, you enjoy my special coffee.

Pratyush – Tell me, where it is?

Aditya – I forgot it at home. Were you here to read that, I thought for dinner again?

Pratyush – Of course not, I came to continue my reading. Do you really think that I'll wet myself in this rain this far to have dinner or coffee? I came to continue my reading.

Aditya – I am so sorry sir, but I forgot it at home.

Pratyush – Come on dude! Don't talk rubbish.

Aditya –I am really sorry sir.

Pratyush – No problem. Let's go. Hurry up.

Aditya – Where?

Pratyush –Your home.

Aditya – Sir it's already 11:40 pm and it is raining as well.

Pratyush –Come on brother, please. I want to read it. I have my car. We'll take the copy and back here. Fine?

Aditya – Ok, if you wish so.

Pratyush – That's the spirit.

(30 minutes later)

Aditya and Pratyush are back in the cafe with the copy. They get themselves seated.

Aditya – Sir coffee?

Pratyush – Sure.

It's 1:30 midnight, Aditya is doing some calculations and budget planning while Pratyush is attentively busy reading the book.

Aditya – Sir you must rest now, it's already 1:30 am. You won't be able to work tomorrow.

Pratyush – I am fine and well I have an off day tomorrow. Can't we spend our night in the cafe only? I mean it's still raining and I want to continue my reading.

Aditya – (hesitatingly) Aa..., Ok. No problem.

The next morning Pratyush left the cafe and didn't come back for two days. Aditya thought that he might not be interested in continuing to read that's why he didn't return.

One usual day Aditya was in the cafe. It was 4 pm in the afternoon. The cafe was almost full of students, couples, and office workers. Some senior citizens were also present. Suddenly Pratyush comes in at Aditya's counter with a file cheerfully. Everyone starts looking at Pratyush. Those who knew him were gathering around to take selfies and autographs. Hearing so much noise outside, Aditya comes out of the kitchen and finds Pratyush.

Pratyush – That's it, everyone. Thank you for all your love, now I have to meet my friend and writer.

Aditya – All good sir?

Pratyush – More than good. I have something for you in that file. There's a pen too.

Aditya – What it is?

Pratyush – Asia's biggest publishing company, P.R.K Publishers Pvt. Ltd wants to launch you and your book, "The Moonlight Smile That Stole My Heart" on International Stage, all over the world. You are the new superstar in the market Aditya. Congratulations Bro.

Aditya – (shocked) But sir...!

Pratyush – You deserve it, brother. Your book made me your fan.

(Everyone is standing and clapping for Aditya. The students are hooting for him.)

Aditya – Sorry, I can't believe this.

(Pratyush pinches Aditya)

Pratyush – I know it was a dream but now it has become your reality my friend.

(Pratyush hugs Aditya)

Chapter - 11

The Superstar Aditya

The release of Aditya's book, "The Moonlight Smile That Stole My Heart" came out thrashing all the records as it registered sales of around 2 million rupees in the opening week of August, 92% of libraries in India by the time had the book in bulks. Aditya was all over, from press to newspaper, from magazines to shows. Every youngster had Aditya's book common in the bag. Although Aditya gained fame and recognition from all over the world, his nature and attitude remained the same, calm, composed, subtle and normal. He doesn't like to attend a lot of press conferences or interviews. However, he does like to attend collages for fun questioning sessions with students nearly of his own age. Pratyush and Aditya usually spend time together. Pratyush takes him to shows, parties, and some time for drives as well.

Everything was going like a dream for Aditya, but now this dream was turning into greatness. On the eve of 28th August, Aditya was nominated for one of the highest international literary awards and that is the "International Dublin Literary Award" He might not have won that, but he won the hearts of millions around the world with his very own story. Day by day Aditya's book was achieving recognition at the global stage but Pratyush thought that the process needs to speed up and so he planned foreign tours to England, Australia, and Canada. But Aditya wasn't interested in visiting foreign places as of now, so he denied. Aditya still runs the cafe as earlier and lives in the same house, alone and lonely as earlier. The only difference being is that now he has more work to do in the cafe. Pratyush helps him out in his cafe sometimes. Aditya's 55% earnings go to various NGOs and Government Help Institutions. Pratyush is very upset with Aditya's decision of coming to foreign tours.

One day when Aditya was at home, the doorbell rang and Aditya opened the door. On opening the door, Aditya saw an American young lady smiling at him. He welcomed her in.

Aditya – Your good name ma'am?

Julie – Myself Julie Johnson. I am from St. Parker School, New York. I need your help, sir.

Aditya – First of all don't say, sir. You can call me Aditya and before you tell me how can I help you, I shall bring coffee for both of us.

Julie – Sure sir. Well, you are way more humble than I thought and heard.

Aditya – Oh! That's really nice to hear.

(5 minutes later)

Aditya brings the coffee.

Aditya –Your coffee.

Julie – Thank you, sir, I mean Aditya.

Aditya – (chuckles) Now tell me, how I can help you.

Julie – Sure. Actually, I run a small school for children of age group 5 to 18, from primary to secondary school.

Aditya – Means you run your own school?

Julie – Yes, a small one, free of cost, for providing education to poor classed children. Would you like to see some photos of my school? I always carry my album in the phone.

Aditya – You are so young, maybe of my age and you are already doing such great work. That's really great. I would love to see the photos.

(Julie is showing the photos of her school and of some functions to Aditya and he is enjoying them.)

(5 minutes later)

Aditya – (smiling) Such a beautiful and cute family of students you have.

Julie – (sadly) Thank you, but I'll have to close the school sooner anytime.

Aditya – (surprisingly) But why?

Julie – The land on which the school was set up was on lease but before I could pay the lease amount, some people took over the land by using unfair tricks and they are pressurizing me to close the school.

Aditya – Didn't you complain to the police?

Julie – Nothing happened. They are local politicians.

Aditya – That's really upsetting. How can I help you with this?

Julie – I promised the children that I will give them a memorable farewell especially to the senior ones as they would now move to colleges. So I thought that if you could just visit our school and spend some time with them. It would be the best farewell they could ever imagine of, most of them have read your book. They are your biggest fans.

Aditya – I really appreciate the idea, ma'am. But I

need some time to think because you know very well now how far America is.

Julie – Just a few hours away.

Aditya – (chuckles) Actually I don't visit foreign countries so I need time to think.

Julie – No problem Aditya. You listened to my request that's more than enough for me. I have my flight at night so here is my number. You can call me if you ever wish to visit America. It was so nice meeting you, you are such a great person.

Aditya – Sure ma'am. It was my pleasure too.

Julie – And one more thing, I want something from you and without getting that, I won't leave this place.

Aditya – What?

Julie – Your autograph and a selfie.

Aditya – (chuckles) Sure.

(30 minutes later)

Aditya calls Pratyush and asks him to come to his house. Pratyush on reaching Aditya's house gets a huge surprise when he finds Aditya packing his bags with two tickets been kept on the table for him and Pratyush.

Aditya – Pack your bags. We are leaving for America.

Pratyush – Seriously? How did you change your mind?

Aditya – A lady came and manipulated my mind. I am going for a visit in her school.

Pratyush – I don't care what the purpose is. You are coming that's the best part.

Aditya – What are you waiting for? Go pack up your bag.

Pratyush – Oh! Yes of course.

Chapter - 12

Destiny's Game of Love

It's the beautiful city of New York. The sun rises as the stars go down but what makes Aditya happier is the freshness in the air of New York which gives birth to thousands of stories daily that might not have started in New York but reaches their destination in this amazing city of dreams.

Aditya's chief guest appearance at the school is tomorrow morning, so he's in his hotel room and making continuous phone calls to some government officials of New York. God knows for what?

You know why friendship is the purest form of love because it is not bound by limits of benefits. Pratyush might not show his concern for Aditya much but he wants his happiness more than anyone and so he started visiting various dance academies as soon as they reached New York. So that Aditya's incomplete story has its perfect end. But unfortunately, his efforts are going in vain, maybe because she is not here.

The next morning, over 500 students of St. Jarvin School raised their voices in amusement when Aditya entered their campus. There were clapping and cheers all over the building. Aditya didn't take the stage for addressing the students; in fact, he sat between them on one of the chairs and talked to each of them personally. He played small games with the juniors and then started answering the question of the senior students in the library. This was how the Question and Answer session went.

Student 1 – Sir, why did you choose this title, "The Moonlight smile That Stole My Heart"?

Aditya – (smiling) Because when she used to smile at night in that twinkling ray of the moon, I felt another level of inner peace. It was a new refreshing feeling for me. If I had to say it in a filmy romantic way then I would say that her smile stole my heart everytime.

Student 2 – Looks like sir got emotional.

Aditya – (chuckles) Maybe, yes.

Student 3 – Sir was it love at first sight?

Aditya – There is no such thing in this duplicate world my friend. Until and unless you love someone by heart by his or her nature, there is no love. I love her because she was humble by nature, cute by actions, trustworthy, and most important thing, she made me realize what it means to live life.

Student 4 – Sir, you said you 'love her' means you still love her even after months?

Aditya – (smiling sadly) Yeah..

Student 5 – Can we assume your love story is incomplete?

Aditya – Every story is complete in itself. This is not a movie where a happy ending is certain. All the love stories are not meant to be completed that way.

Student 6 – Why didn't you propose to her?

Aditya – Fear and lack of courage. Fear of losing a friend.

Student 7 – Do you feel lonely now?

Aditya – Practically not but yes somewhere inside.

Student 8 – How would you describe love?

Aditya – A special feeling for someone which is indescribable. When you think of someone else before yourself when you do things which you don't like for the person you love. When you laugh and fight on small things. I believe that if you seriously love someone then go gather some courage and just confess keeping your ego aside. Maybe destiny has something for you as well.

Student 9 – Why did you write a book on this?

Aditya – To keep our memories alive forever. Before

I leave, how many of you have started your exam preparations?

Student 10 - What's the point, sir? We won't be able to give an exam in this school.

Aditya – I told you I brought a gift for everyone. So, that's the gift.

Student 10 – Didn't get it, sir?

Aditya – You will give your exams here and no one is going to take your school from you. This land belongs to the students of St. Jarvin School forever.

With this line, the campus of St. Jarvin School was filled with happiness and cheers. Everyone danced in the feeling of happiness and Aditya standing on one side smiled towards Miss Julie.

Aditya's book rocked the international market. He will leave for India tomorrow.

After returning from school, Aditya went on a drive with Pratyush who was feeling sad because he was not able to find Ahana. After returning, when Aditya was walking in the park late at night to get some fresh air, he met an Indian girl who was cute and funny. At first, the girl didn't know who Aditya was but she got to know when she was reading his book in the park and Aditya saw her.

Aditya – Would you mind if I see your book for a second?

Drishti – Sure. Have you read this? If not then you must. It's so touching and peaceful.

Aditya – (laughing) I have read it.

Drishti – Why are you laughing? Your accent tells me you are an Indian.

Aditya – Oh! Yes. I am from India.

Drishti – Have you shifted recently?

Aditya –No I came here for some work. I am a writer by profession.

Drishti – Oh! I see. Your good name?

Aditya – Aditya Sharma. Yours?

Drishti – Drishti Singh.

Aditya – Ok, bye. You continue your book.

Drishti continues her reading but suddenly something strikes her mind and she turns back to Aditya.

Drishti – Excuse me. Can you tell me which book have you written?

Aditya – (smiling) The one you are holding.

Drishti – (shocked) My goodness. You are the writer Aditya Sharma? I can't believe my luck.

Aditya – (laughing) Calm down I am Aditya Sharma, not Elon Musk.

Drishti – Who wants to meet Elon Musk when you are standing in front?

Drishti and Aditya start talking for an hour where Aditya is telling her the story personally and Drishti is keen on listening to him tell his story himself. She hasn't completed the book but now the whole story is known to her in brief. She was paying special attention when Aditya was describing Ahana and her nature and how he fell in love with her.

Drishti – You remind me of someone I know personally when you talk about Ahana.

Aditya – Who?

Drishti – You'll laugh if I will tell you, so better leave it.

They both go home after plenty of talks. Drishti lives in a small house with her friend who doesn't like reading books. Drushti is thinking something very deeply while looking at the book. Whereas on the other hand, Aditya is packing his bags as there is a change in plan and they are leaving today only, in an hour or two.

Drishti's anxiety was too much for her to handle so she woke her friend up who was sleeping soundly.

Drishti – Ahana wake up. Please, I have some confusion.

Ahana – (in sleepy voice) What?

Drishti – First sit properly. It's important.

Ahana – Ok, fine. Now tell.

Drishti – You told me that you fell in love with a boy who lived with you in India. You were good friends, right?

Ahana – Yes, but why are you asking all this at this time?

Drishti – What was his name? Tell me fast, his full name. Maybe my guess is right.

Ahana – You are talking about Adi?

Drishti – Yes, what is his full name?

Ahana – Aditya Sharma.

Drishti – Was he a writer?

Ahana – Yes, he used to write books but none of them were published. I wish he becomes one day.

Drishti – (shocked) My goodness, this is what we call

the game of destiny.

Ahana –I don't know what you are talking about. I am going to sleep and you should also take a rest.

Drishti – No, don't sleep. Do you still love him?

Ahana –Forget it Drishti.

Drishti – Answer me. Do you still love him?

Ahana – Yes, of course. But why are asking all this?

Drishti – Wait here.

(Drishti brings the book and shows it to her)

Drishti – The Moonlight Smile That Stole My Heart, is the book I have been reading for a week and it's writer is none other than Aditya Sharma.

Ahana – What are you trying to say, that this is written by the same Adi whom I love? Get back to reality Drishti, Aditya Sharma, this name is the most common name for boys in India.

Drishti – What if I prove you?

Ahana – And how are you gonna do this?

Drishti – Turn to any page and read it for sometime. If you don't find the story familiar with yours, then just throw it away.

Ahana – How will I understand the story if I don't

read it from start?

Drishti – You will, because my heart says that this is your story. Go ahead and prove me right.

Ahana – Fine.

Ahana starts reading from page number 27 and after a minute her eyes were filled with tears. However she controls them, she then turned another page and after randomly reading 5-6 pages, she broke out crying loudly hugging Drishti.

Drishti – I knew this. See my instincts are great.

Ahana – I can't believe that he wrote a book on our story. I never thought that he too loves me. Well, these things are of no use now, I can't tell him what I feel for him now, our paths are different on the two ends of the world.

Drishti – Get ready and come with me.

Ahana – But where and why?

Drishti – To complete this story. I have a chance to do this and so I'll put up everything in bringing it to its deserving end. The finishing chapter will be written by me. Come on get up. I am so excited.

Drishti takes Ahana to the hotel which was nearer

to the park where she met Aditya. On enquiring about the reception, they got to know that Aditya and Pratyush have already checked out of the hotel. Outside the hotel, a black car passes by the side of Drishti, and fortunately, she looked in the car. Destiny has a lot of levels to play with Ahana and this is certainly the most difficult one. Drishti quickly stopped the cab and pulled Ahana in. On reaching the airport, they took a sigh of relief when they got to know that the flight from New York to India is late by 15 minutes. Ahana and Drishti are searching for Aditya all around the airport but every effort is worthless when god is writing your story.

Ahana and Aditya are just a few meters away from each other but they won't see each other if it's not written in their chapter. Aditya's pen falls on the ground for which he bents down and Ahana turns towards him but can only see his back, Aditya's pen who has been telling this story all the way finally helped Aditya find his love. A loud call from Aditya, "Ahana!" and that moment comes when the two of them see each other. Drishti and Pratyush are watching them keenly and then comes the most awaited moment when Ahana runs towards Aditya and they both kiss each other and finally the book "The Moonlight Smile that stole My Heart" got to its perfect end.

- KUSHAL SINGH

Epilogue

22 Years Later

19th July 2042

It's the occasion of Shantanu's 17th birthday. He cuts the cake and firstly feeds his loving father Aditya and then Ahana. Ahana gives him a watch as gift. Shantanu takes it cheerfully and hugs Ahana. He then asks Aditya, "Dad you promised me that you would give me your most precious thing which I have been eagerly waiting to see". Aditya takes out a pen from his pocket and pins it in Shantanu's shirt's pocket. Shantanu was filled with joy on receiving the pen which narrated his parent's love story.

The End

About The Author

Kushal Singh

Kushal Singh is a 16-year-old Indian scriptwriter, novelist, and motivational speaker. He writes film scripts and novels specializing in romance and suspense thrillers. He published his first book at the age of 14. His motivational show- "Zindagi Aur Hum" is also very famous all over India. His recently written romantic novel- "The Moonlight Smile that Stole my Heart" and the romantic suspense thriller- "It's a Secret: The Unrevealed love story" are some famous works currently.

Books By This Author

The Inspiration

Attractive lovely rhyming poems that will give every thought wings and will take you to the mirror of world and its reality. How people win and lose from the societal false thoughts. Steps taken by people in conditions. The sense of wrong and right judged by others. Some situations faced by people and the dealing of emotions at times.

The Hidden Battle For The Nation

Thieves in past..patriots in present. The story is set in the country of Sweden and Russia when the relation between the countries were on extreme bitterness. Read how two thieves Kevin and Ross come up for their country when everyone was terrified for the suspicious and extremely dangerous work i.e. of being a spy in order to save their country. Full of action packed animated images to take you to the background. A lot of genre supporting book especially patriotism, friendship and love.

Mark Vendor And The Crime Mystery

The novel is about a boy, Mark who is new to school and is very smart with a detective brain. See how he saves his girlfriend's life and of many other girls who are being victims of a crime mystery at his own school.Mark, a boy with extra detective powers can only expose the crime squad in his school

www.ingramcontent.com/pod-product-compliance
Lightning Source LLC
La Vergne TN
LVHW041134150826
845673LV00007B/2322